Praise for Rebirth of the Gangster

"Standal has great range as a writer..
This is one of those series that really
benefits from a reread of what came before...
Juan Romera's art on this book is a perfect fit.
The series...gives off a definite **Walking Dead** vibe."
-Fanbase Press

"The whole comic is starting to feel like **The Wire**...
and, certainly, the clean, crisp simple line-work of
Juan Romera reads like a storyboard with clearly defined and
distinguishable characters...Romera's artwork reminds us of
David Mazzuchelli on **Batman: Year One** crossed with the late
and lamented Darwyn Cooke, all bold but simple brush strokes
and strong shadow work giving life to each panel."
-Pipedream Comics

"**Rebirth of the Gangster** is a fantastic noir series with
a cool, nostalgic art style and an engaging crime story....
I like the diversity that the comic creators are going for...We
have gotten the perspective of a black male in crime-related
situations, a white male in crime-related situations, and
now we are getting the perspective of a Latina female...
C.J. Standal crafts these characters in a believable, down to
earth and empathetic way, without parodies or caricatures.
C.J. is good at breaking down people, and situations,
to where we feel for them and can even imagine
ourselves in their situations."
-Comic Booked

"So, good story? Check.
Diverse cast? Check.
Solid art? Check.
This is a comic to check out and support."
-Graphic Policy

ALSO BY CJ STANDAL

Rebirth of the Gangster
Act 1: Meet the Family
Act 2: What's Old is New
Act 3: A Family Affair
Act 4: Inheritance

B.A.E. Wulf
The Shadow Over Innsmarch
The Haunting of Chinatown

Nonfiction
*Outside the Panels: Comics,
the Classroom, and the Creative Life*

Act 3: A Family Affair

CJ STANDAL
WRITER

JUAN ROMERA
ARTIST

Rebirth of the Gangster Act 3: A Family Affair. Rebirth of the Gangster © 2020 CJ Standal

Contact:
website: cjstandalproductions.com
Twitter: @cj_standal
email: cjstandal@gmail.com

Rebirth of the Gangster
Act 3: A Family Affair

by

CJ Standal

ISBN: 9780578696737

Book design: CJ Standal

Published by CJ Standal Productions
814 Nancy Ln.
Madison, WI 53704

Distributed by
Ingram Spark
1 Ingram Blvd.
La Verne, TN 3708624

A Family Affair: Linda

I'M TELLING YOU, THAT RANDY SMITH IS UP TO NO GOOD, ESPECIALLY WITH THAT HUNTER GUY HE'S BEEN TALKING TO DURING VISITING HOURS.

YEAH, I AGREE WITH YOU, BUT DO YOU HAVE ANY PROOF, ANYTHING I CAN USE?

...NO.

I CAN'T HELP YOU YET WITHOUT PROOF. BUT KEEP YOUR EYES AND EARS OPEN.

...OK.

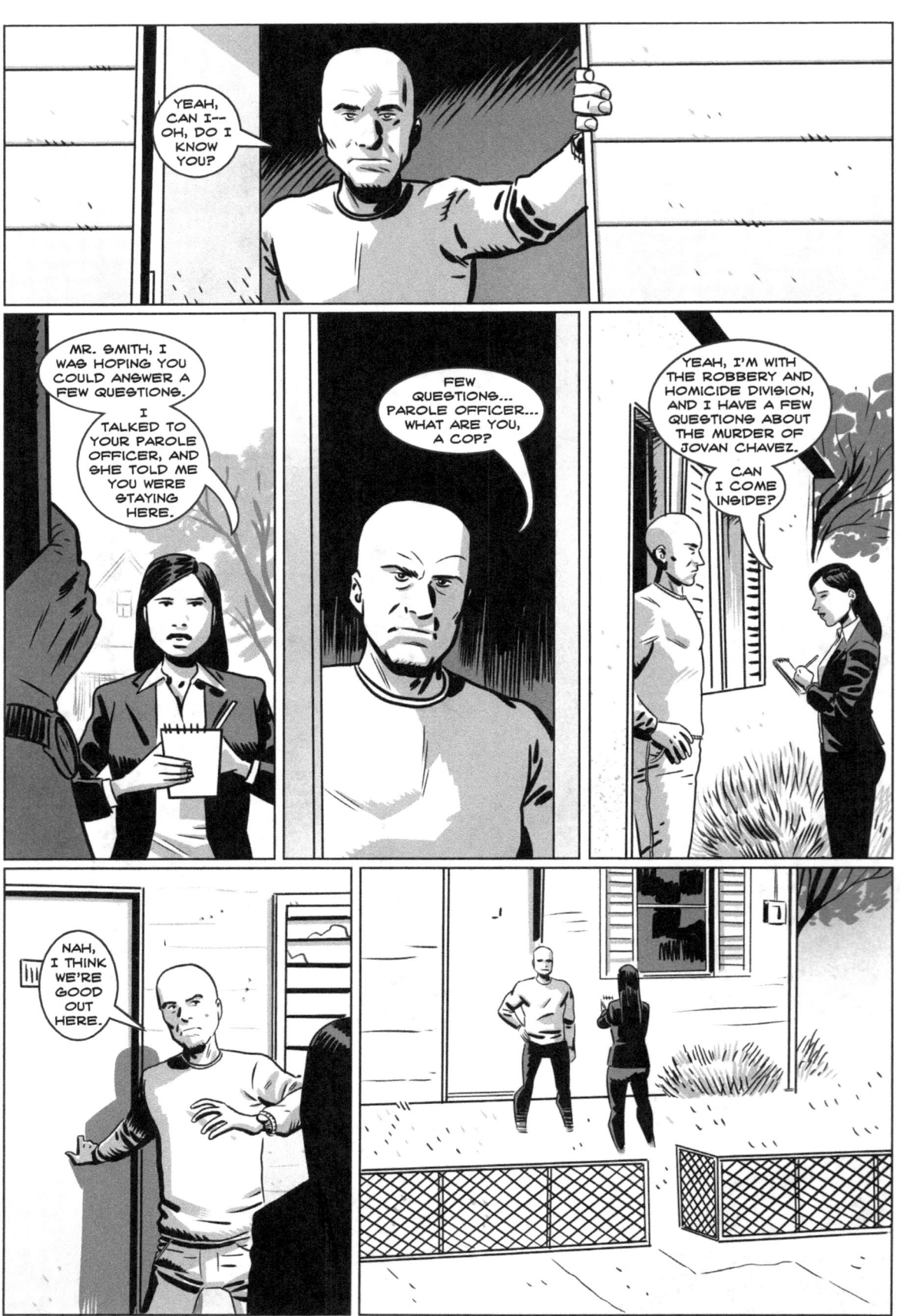

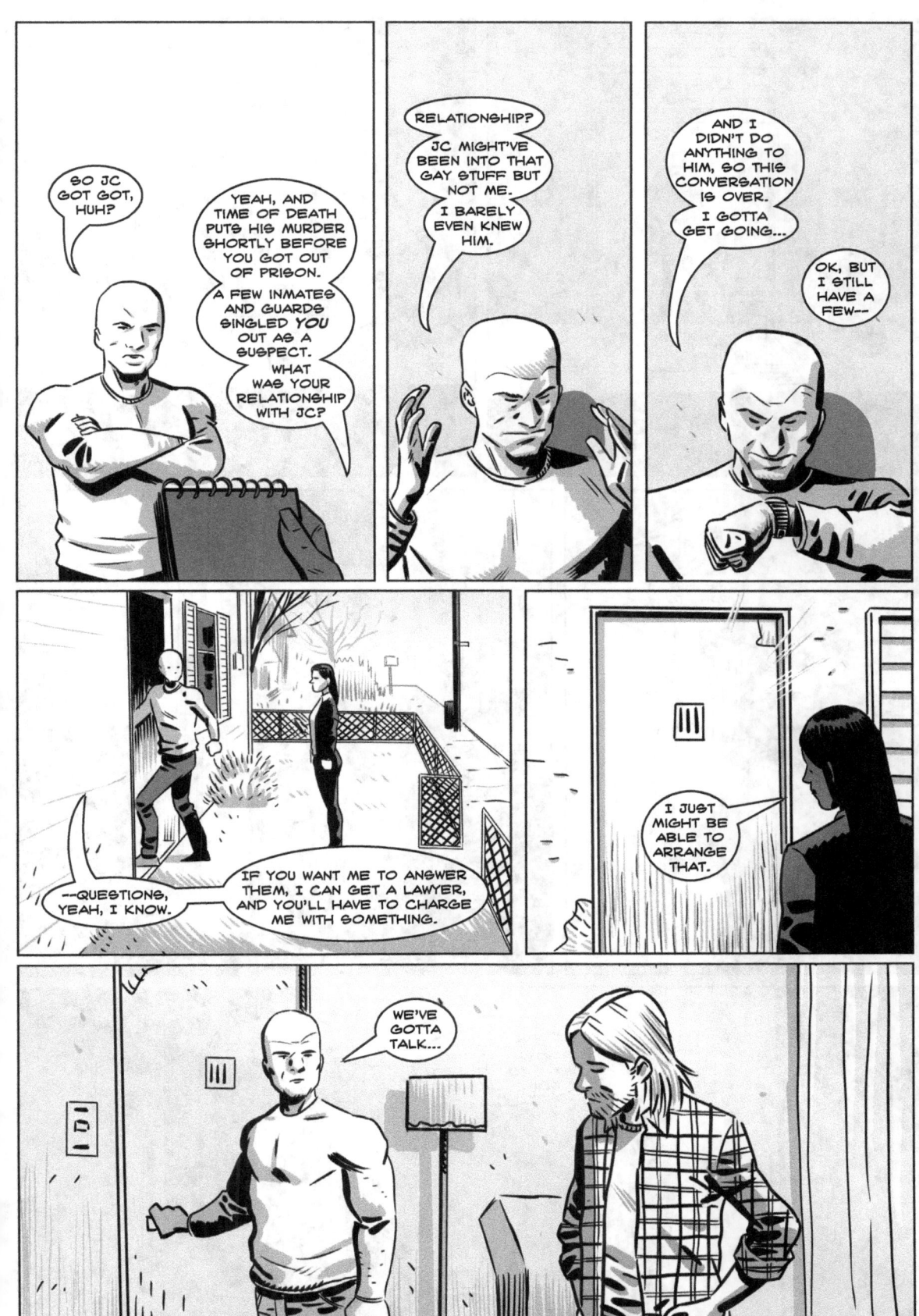

HEY, MARCUS, GOT A SEC?

I'VE GOT SOMETHING I WANT TO ASK YOU.

IT'S ABOUT SOME OF THE WORK YOU'VE BEEN DOING LATELY.

SLOPPY, SKETCHY WORK THAT DOESN'T MAKE SENSE TO ME.

SKETCHY... WHAT, UH, WHAT DO YOU MEAN?

OH, IT'S NOT JUST ONE THING.

A LOT OF YOUR WORK HAS BEEN SLOPPY LATELY, BUT THE THING I'M NOT QUITE SURE OF IS WHY YOU GAVE RANDY SMITH A PLEA BARGAIN.

OH, I'VE JUST BEEN HAVING SOME PERSONAL ISSUES-- DACARA BROKE UP WITH ME.

THAT'S ACTUALLY WHY I DID THAT PLEA: HIS ORIGINAL SENTENCE WAS TOO HARSH.

(I THINK I WAS TAKING MY ANGER AT DACARA OUT ON HIM, YOU KNOW?)

...

YEAH, I KNOW HOW IT IS.

JUST LET ME KNOW IF YOU WANT TO TALK.

OR LET ME KNOW IF YOU WANT SOMEONE TO DOUBLE-CHECK FOR ANY MISTAKES LIKE THAT, OK?

I'LL KEEP THAT IN MIND, THANKS.

RELATIONSHIP TROUBLES...

YEAH, SURE.

--AND SO THAT'S WHERE WE STAND.

GLAD YOU'RE HERE, BIG D: I CAN GUESS WHAT HUNTER'LL SAY, BUT I THOUGHT YOU MIGHT WANT TO WEIGH IN, SINCE YOU'RE TIED UP IN THIS TOO.

I DIDN'T SIGN UP FOR ANY OF THIS.

AND I HAD NOTHING TO DO WITH YOUR CRAZY ANTICS.

YEAH, NEITHER DID I, SO WHY SHOULD WE HELP YOU CLEAN UP *YOUR* MESS?

TRUE, BUT YOU BOTH HELPED ME GET OUT, BLACKMAILING ONE OF THIS CITY'S FINEST CITIZENS... NEED I GO ON?

I COULD, IF THE COPS PUT THOSE CUFFS ON ME.

OK...

WHAT DO YOU WANT TO DO?

THAT'S MORE LIKE IT!

I WAS THINKING--

WE COULD TAKE HER OUT...

HA! LET'S COVER UP ONE BODY BY PILING ANOTHER ON TOP OF IT.

HOW THE FUCK'LL THAT HELP US?

SEE WHAT I'VE BEEN DEALING WITH? ASSHOLE THINKS POURING GAS ON A FIRE IS THE SOLUTION TO EVERYTHING.

YEAH, I CAN'T DO THAT AND RISK GOING BACK TO JAIL. I'VE GOT A GOOD THING WITH LIZZETH, AND I CAN'T MESS IT UP.

THANKS FOR MEETING ME HERE. I WAS SICK OF STAYING AT MY PLACE. HOPEFULLY THIS IS FAR ENOUGH AWAY FROM ANYONE YOU KNOW.

YEAH, HOPEFULLY. I DON'T KNOW IF I CAN DO THIS AGAIN, BUT I'LL GIVE IT A SHOT.

SORRY I'M SO LATE. WORK'S BEEN HECTIC.

...NO PROBLEM. I JUST GOT HERE.

WHAT'S THE SPECIAL OCCASION? YOU'RE NORMALLY TOO BUSY TO MEET UP FOR LUNCH.

WELL, AS ALWAYS, IT'S ABOUT WORK.

THERE'S SOMETHING I DIDN'T TELL YOU, SOMETHING I SHOULD HAVE...

I DON'T WANT THIS TO SOUND LIKE AN EXCUSE, BUT--

I'M AN ADDICT, AND I'VE DONE SOME HORRIBLE THINGS. IF I COULD TAKE THEM BACK, YOU KNOW I WOULD.

BUT I'M NOT THAT PERSON ANYMORE. I'M CLEAN NOW, AND YOU KNOW I'D NEVER DO ANYTHING LIKE THAT AGAIN.

THAT'S IT? JUST, "I'M AN ADDICT, SO JUST FORGIVE ME"?

I'M GONNA NEED MORE THAN THAT.

DON'T LAUGH AT ME, YOUNG MAN! I'M ONLY TRYING TO PROTECT--

YEAH, YEAH, YEAH--PROTECT THIS FAMILY.

THAT DIDN'T QUITE SEEM TO BE ON YOUR MIND WHEN I SAW YOU HAVING DINNER WITH (HOW SHOULD I PUT THIS?) YOUR BOY TOY.

WHAT? THAT, THAT'S NONE OF YOUR BUSINESS.

YOU DON'T, YOU DON'T KNOW WHAT WAS REALLY GOING ON.

JUST LIKE YOU DON'T KNOW WHAT'S REALLY GOING ON WITH HUNTER.

OH, I KNOW A LOT MORE THAN YOU GIVE ME CREDIT FOR.

AND I'M TAKING CARE OF IT--I DON'T NEED YOU SWOOPING IN TO SAVE THE DAY.

...

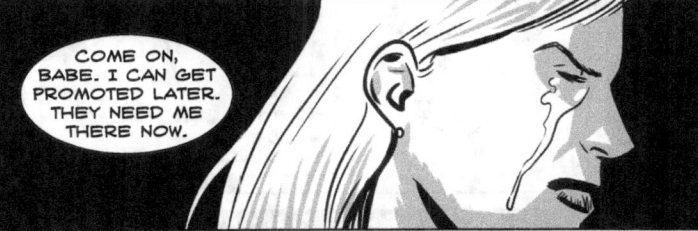

HEY, HON, HOW WAS WORK?

EH, YOU KNOW, SOME KIDS WANT TO DO RIGHT AND SOME KIDS BEING LITTLE SHITS.

HOW'S THE JOB HUNT GOING?

SAME OLD, SAME OLD: I POUNDED THE PAVEMENT A LITTLE BUT DIDN'T GET ANY BITES.

FROM WHERE I'M STANDING, IT DOESN'T LOOK LIKE YOU DID MUCH. AND MAYBE THAT'S BECAUSE YOU ALREADY GOT A JOB, ONE YOU DON'T WANT ME TO KNOW ABOUT.

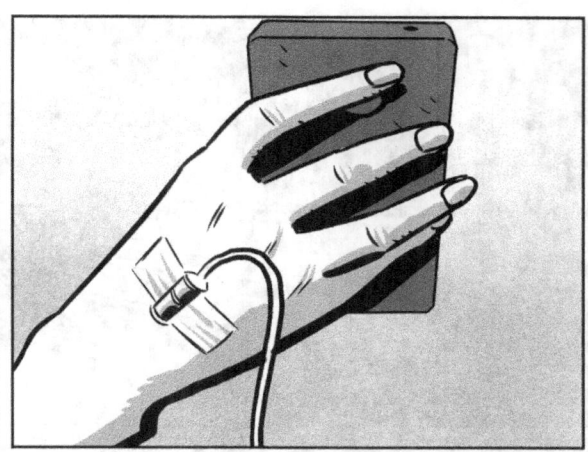
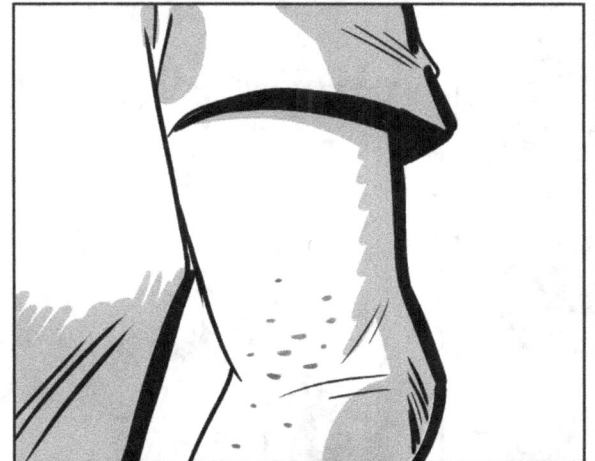

YOU WANTED TO MEET?

I DON'T KNOW WHY I CAME AFTER YOU WERE BEING SUCH A PUSSY, BUT HERE I AM.

THANKS. YEAH, I WANTED TO MEET.

LIZZETH JUST BROKE IT OFF, SO--

--SO YOU THOUGHT YOU'D COME WHINE TO ME.

I KNEW I SHOULDN'T HAVE COME--

NO, YOU DON'T GET IT. SHE WAS THE REASON I WAS "PUSSYING OUT".

WE SHOULD TALK ABOUT YOUR PLAN AGAIN.

I'M NOT SAYING WE SHOULD TAKE THE COP OUT...

BUT WE SHOULD DO *SOMETHING*...

A Family Affair: Lorena

SMITH, RANDY
CASE FILE

NOTHING, NOTHING, NOTHING...

HMM...

Juvenile Records

9/15/95--Assault/Altercation with Hunter Thompson, Thompson the instigator.

2/12/96--Assault/Altercation with Hunter Thompson, Thompson the instigator.

5/27/96--Assault/Altercation with Hunter Thor Thompson the instigator.

9/10/96--Assault/Altercation with Hunter Th Thompson the instigator.

WHY WOULD HE BE WORKING WITH HIS CHILDHOOD BULLY?

PHOOOOO

SHIT! ANN'S GOING TO KILL ME.

THAT IS, *IF* SHE'S SPEAKING TO ME.

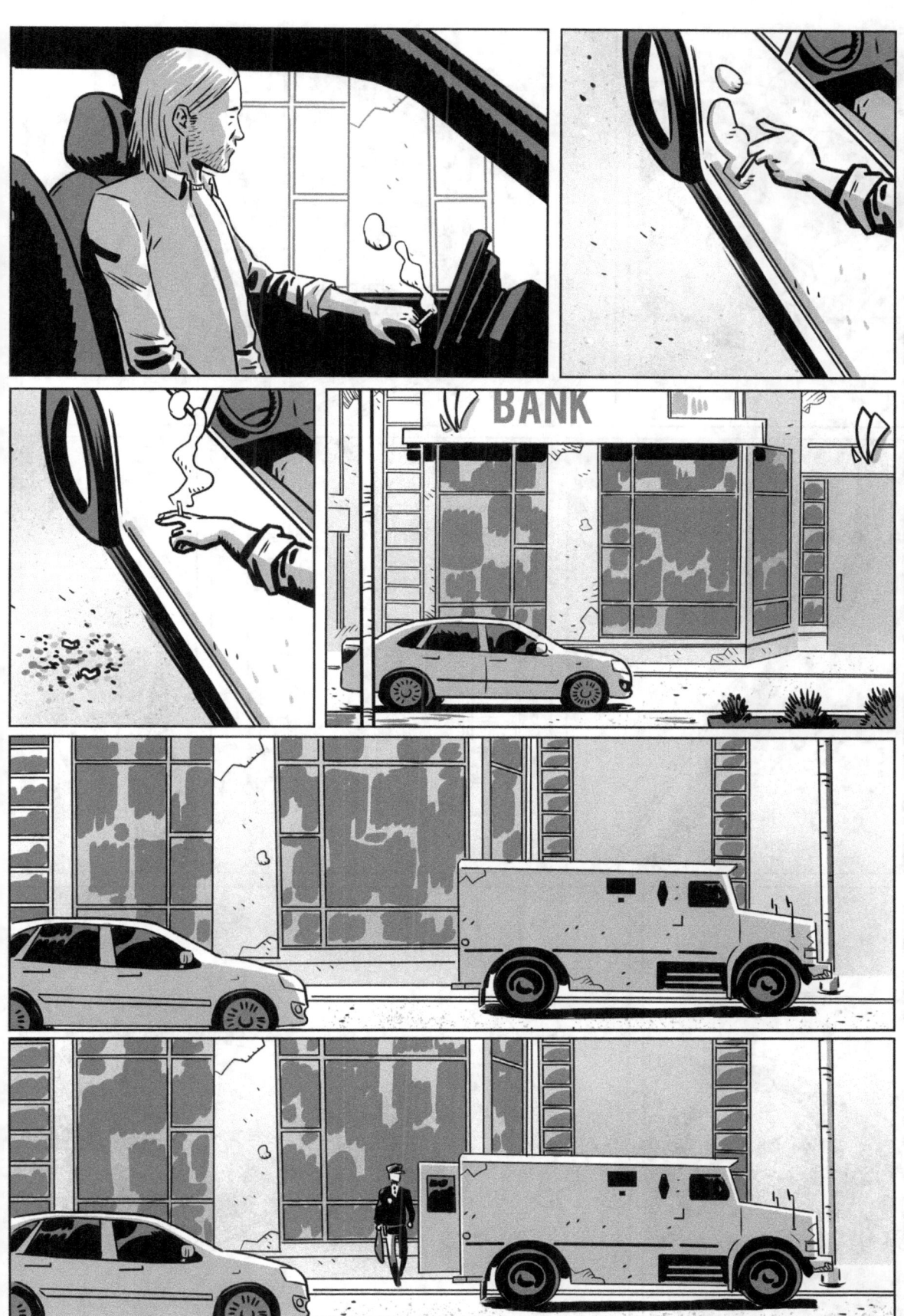

COME ON, OUTTA THE WAY!

PAY DIRT.

I'M SURPRISED YOU WANTED TO COME BACK HERE, YOU KNOW, AFTER LAST TIME...

WELL, I WANTED TO SHOW I CAN GET PAST IT.

HOPEFULLY YOU CAN TOO?

OF COURSE, THAT'S WHAT *WE DO*--PUT THE PAST MISTAKES BEHIND US.

WHAT'S UP?

I'VE BEEN DOING CHEMO.

AND I NEED YOUR HELP.

OH SHIT! I'M SO SORRY.

HOW'RE YOU HOLDING UP?

THANKS. EH--IT'S ROUGH.

AND --I KNOW I SHOULDN'T--BUT I'M THINKING OF USING AGAIN.

HOW WILL *THAT* HELP?

I KNOW IT WON'T.

BUT THAT DOESN'T STOP ME FROM WANTING IT, YOU KNOW.

BUT IT'S NOT REALLY THE CHEMO THAT MAKES ME WANT TO USE AGAIN...

I TOLD HUNTER THE TRUTH ABOUT MY PAST MISTAKES AND..

SO...
WE'RE BACK
HERE AGAIN.

I THOUGHT
WE'D MADE
PROGRESS--I
HAD A GREAT
TIME AT LUNCH
WITH YOU.

I KNOW,
I DID TOO.
BUT MY SON WAS
ACROSS THE STREET,
AND I CAN'T RISK
ANOTHER CALL LIKE
THAT. I'M SURE YOU
UNDERSTAND,
BABE.

...YEAH.

HEY, BABE! I'M HOME A LITTLE EARLY FOR A CHANGE.

I HAD A FEW THINGS I COULD'VE FINISHED AT THE PRECINCT, BUT I THOUGHT,

"IT'S BEEN TOO LONG SINCE I HUNG OUT WITH MI AMOR."

HOW WAS YOUR DAY?

...FINE.

THANKS FOR MEETING ME. YOU'LL BE GLAD TO HEAR THIS—

WE'RE READY TO MOVE TO THE NEXT PHASE OF THE PLAN.

ACTUALLY, THERE'S SOMETHING WE WANT TO DO FIRST.

YEAH, WE CIRCLED BACK TO MY IDEA...

REALLY? DENNIS, HOW'D HE TALK YOU INTO THIS STUPID SHIT?

HE DIDN'T TALK ME INTO ANYTHING.

WE NEED TO DO THIS-- I CAN'T HAVE HER TALKING TO LIZZETH.

...

WELL, I'M OUT.

LET ME KNOW IF YOU WANT BACK IN ON THE PLAN THAT WILL GET US MONEY AND REVENGE:

BUT ONLY IF YOU COME TO YOUR SENSES.

WHAT'VE YOU GOT FOR ME, MARCUS?

AND WHY DO YOU LOOK SO HAPPY?

I WAS THINKING OF MY RECENT WORK'S...WELL, YOU KNOW.

AND SO I WENT BACK TO SOME OLD CASES TO SEE IF THERE WAS SOMETHING I'D MISSED. I DON'T KNOW IF YOU REMEMBER DEVONTE ROBINSON'S CASE.

KID HANGING WITH SOME OTHERS WHO WERE HOLDING.

MAINTAINED HE WAS IN THE WRONG PLACE AT THE WRONG TIME.

YEAH, WHAT ABOUT IT?

WELL, TURNS OUT ONE OF THE REPORTS SAYS ROBINSON WAS ONLY IN THE HOUSE FOR A MINUTE BEFORE THE BUST.

AND HE HAD NO CONTRABAND ON HIM.

DON'T KNOW WHY ROBINSON'S LAWYER DIDN'T SAY ANYTHING.

YOU KNOW, PROBABLY HAD 10 MINUTES TO PREP THE CASE.

BUT WHY'S THIS OUR PROBLEM?

IT ISN'T... YET.

BUT I KNOW HE'S APPEALING THE CASE--WITH A DECENT LAWYER THIS TIME--AND I THINK WE SHOULD GET AHEAD OF THIS.

THIS AGREEMENT COULD SAVE US SOME FACE.

...OK, I'LL LOOK INTO IT.

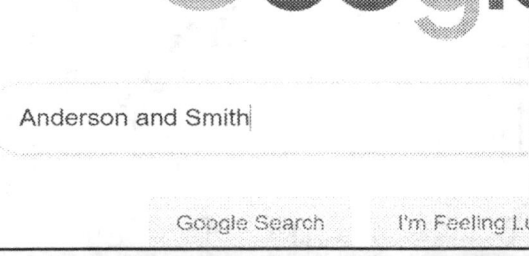

Anderson and Smith

Google Search   I'm Feeling L...

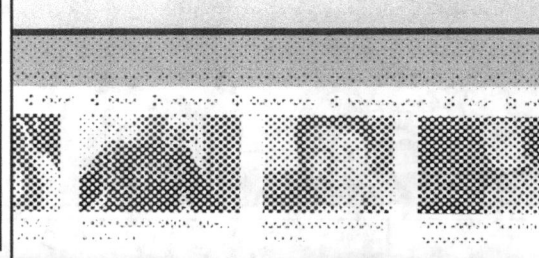

WHAT?!?

Young Curtis Thompson with the late John Anderson and Robert Smith

HI, IS MARCUS THOMPSON STILL THERE?

CAN YOU TELL HIM LORENA SANCHEZ IS COMING BY IN A COUPLE MINUTES?

HE'LL KNOW WHAT IT'S ABOUT.

I WAS WONDERING IF YOU KNEW ANYTHING ABOUT THIS PICTURE.

NO...I'VE NEVER SEEN THESE PEOPLE WITH MY DAD BEFORE.

WHO ARE THEY?

JOHN ANDERSON AND ROBERT SMITH-- TWO CRIMINALS WHO WERE SUSPECTED IN A BIG ROBBERY--

BUT THEY DIED UNDER SUSPICIOUS CIRCUMSTANCES, BEFORE THEY COULD BE CHARGED WITH ANYTHING.

I DON'T KNOW WHAT TO TELL YOU.

I KNOW MY DAD HAD A ROUGH BACKGROUND, BUT HE'S PUT THAT ALL BEHIND HIM.

...

REBIRTH Of The GANGSTER

#15

A Family Affair: Dennis

HEY, DAD!

SON! GOOD TO SEE YOU.

MOM.

HONEY. GOOD TO SEE YOU.

YOU'RE A LITTLE LATE. WHERE WERE YOU?

MARCUS! DON'T TALK TO YOUR FATHER LIKE THAT! HE'S TELLING YOU THE TRUTH.

OF COURSE YOU'D SAY THAT. BUT WHY SHOULD I BELIEVE YOU, ESPECIALLY AFTER THIS AFTERNOON?

WHAT'S HE TALKING ABOUT, BABE?

NOTHING. *RIGHT*, HONEY?

...YEAH, NOTHING.

I TOLD YOU WE NEEDED TO DO SOMETHING ABOUT MARCUS AND THE ANDERSONS.

YEAH, AND I THOUGHT YOU WERE TAKING CARE OF IT.

YEAH, JUST LIKE I DO ALL THE TIME...

JUST LIKE I DID WITH *HIM* BACK IN THE DAY.

YOU COULDN'T SO I HAD TO.

DON'T ACT LIKE YOU'VE DONE EVERYTHING.

I HAD TO TAKE CARE OF OUR OTHER PROBLEM...

...YOU'RE RIGHT. AND PLACING BLAME DOESN'T HELP US SOLVE THIS.

BUT HOW DO WE?

THOMPSONS! STOP BEING WALLFLOWERS AND JOIN THE PARTY!

...FINE. BUT MAKE IT SHORT.

JUST... FORGET WHAT I'VE DONE.

IT'S NOT ABOUT ME ANYMORE. LET'S TALK ABOUT YOU.

AND WHAT YOU'RE ABOUT TO DO.

I DON'T KNOW THE SPECIFICS, BUT I KNOW YOU'RE GOING AFTER THAT FAMILY.

IT'S NOT GOING TO HELP.

IT'S ONLY GOING TO SUCK YOU IN DEEPER.

UNTIL YOU'RE ALONE.

OR DEAD.

JUST LIKE YOUR DAD.

HEY, DEVONTE, I KNOW IT TOOK AWHILE--

BUT I GOT YOU OUT.

MY MAN! THANKS, BROTHER, THIS MEANS...

SO WHEN DO I GET OUT?

JUST AS SOON AS THEY CLEAR THE PAPERWORK. PROBABLY TOMORROW. BUT--

WHEN YOU GET OUT, THERE'S SOMETHING I WANT YOU TO DO FOR ME.

HEY!

AHHHH!

SHE GOT AWAY!

WE GOTTA GET OUT OF HERE TOO!

A Family Affair: Hunter

YOU LISTENING, HUNTER?

HUH? OH, HOW'D YOUR "BRIGHT IDEA" GO?

THERE WAS A PROBLEM.

AND YOU'RE NOT GOING TO LIKE IT ANY MORE THAN WE DID.

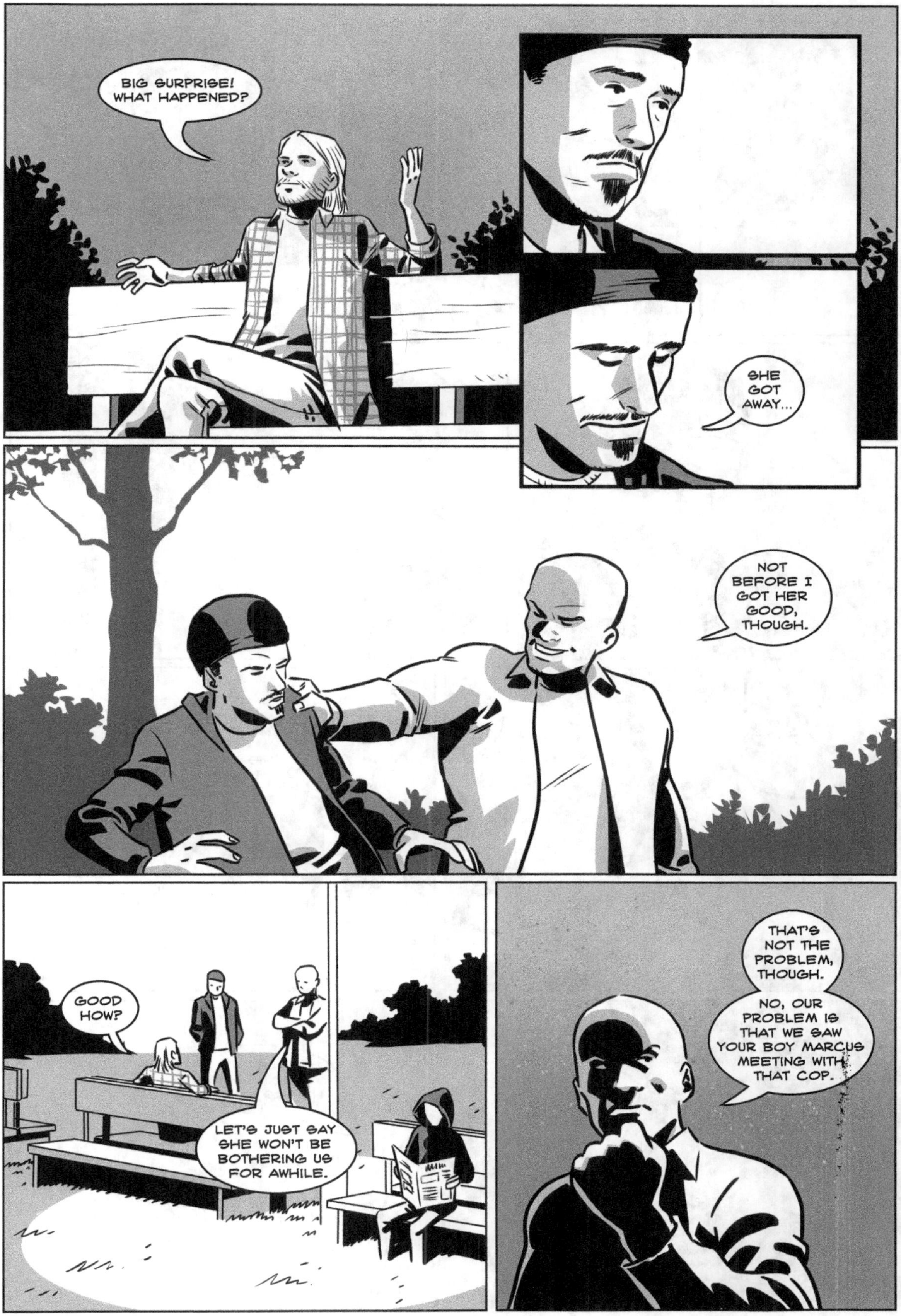

BIG SURPRISE! WHAT HAPPENED?

SHE GOT AWAY...

NOT BEFORE I GOT HER GOOD, THOUGH.

GOOD HOW?

LET'S JUST SAY SHE WON'T BE BOTHERING US FOR AWHILE.

THAT'S NOT THE PROBLEM, THOUGH.

NO, OUR PROBLEM IS THAT WE SAW YOUR BOY MARCUS MEETING WITH THAT COP.

WHAT DO YOU MEAN, MEETING WITH LORENA?

...

EXACTLY WHAT I SAID.

ACTUALLY, WE DIDN'T SEE THEM MEET. JUST HER GOING INTO AND OUT OF HIS OFFICE BUILDING.

IT DOESN'T MATTER. I'M SURE HE WAS TALKING TO HER.

AND WE GOTTA DO SOMETHING ABOUT IT.

HONEY, WHAT HAPPENED? ARE YOU OK?

IT'S NOTHING, JUST A SCRATCH.

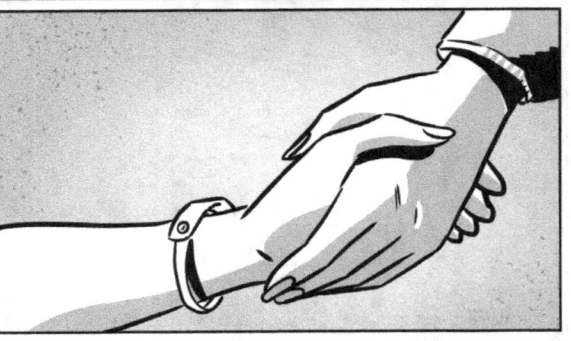

SORRY, MA'AM, BUT WE NEED TO GET HER TO AN OPERATING ROOM.

YOU HAVE TO WAIT OUTSIDE.

BUT--

SEEMS LIKE YOUR WAY OF HANDLING THE BOY DIDN'T WORK.

I DIDN'T DO ANYTHING TO SET HIM OFF. WE ALWAYS KNEW HE MIGHT RESENT US EVEN THOUGH WE NEVER TOLD HIM WHAT WE DID.

THIS IS DIFFERENT THAN ANY OF HIS REBELLIOUS RESENTMENT AS A KID.

YOU DIDN'T LET ANYTHING SLIP, DID YOU?

HE DIDN'T FIND OUT SOMETHING HE SHOULDN'T HAVE, DID HE?

SHE'S LAID UP, AND YOU *STILL* CAN'T LEAVE HER ALONE.

JUST DOING MY JOB.

AHEM. I'LL FOLLOW UP WITH YOU LATER.

SEE YOU, BAYLISS.

THANKS AGAIN FOR MEETING ME FOR A BITE, BETS.

IT'S BEEN TOO LONG, SORRY.

DON'T WORRY ABOUT IT, HONEY.

I KNOW YOU'VE BEEN GOING THROUGH A LOT.

BESIDES, IT'S NOT LIKE YOU'VE NEVER DONE THIS BEFORE.

YOU'VE BEEN LIKE THIS EVER SINCE WE WERE KIDS.

LIKE THAT TIME YOU AND I GOT CAUGHT SHOPLIFTING AT KELLY'S MARKET.

YOU DIDN'T TALK TO ME FOR MONTHS.

AND ONLY BECAUSE I SCORED SOME KILLER STEVIE NICKS TICKETS.

THEY *WERE* KILLER TICKETS.

LIZZETH, BEFORE YOU HANG UP, HEAR ME OUT.

I'VE THOUGHT A LOT ABOUT WHAT YOU SAID, AND I'M READY TO MAKE A CHANGE, I MEAN, *REALLY* MAKE A CHANGE. I CAN'T LOSE YOU.

I JUST WANT TO MEET.

JUST NAME THE TIME AND PLACE.

HUNTER. READY FOR A SHOW?

LET'S CUT THE SHIT.

WHAT WERE YOU DOING TALKING TO THE COP?

NOTHING. SHE JUST HAD A FEW QUESTIONS.

WHAT'D YOU TELL HER?

NOTHING THAT'LL GET YOU INTO TROUBLE, I HOPE?

NO, NOTHING.

SHE SHOWED ME SOME PICTURES, ONES I KNEW NOTHING ABOUT.

BUT YOU MIGHT.

A PICTURE OF MY DAD WITH YOURS.

YOU KNOW MORE THAN YOU'VE BEEN TELLING ME.

HOW DID MY DAD KNOW YOURS?

THEY USED TO WORK TOGETHER.

ON JOBS THAT WERE-- HOW SHOULD I PUT THIS?

LESS THAN LEGAL.

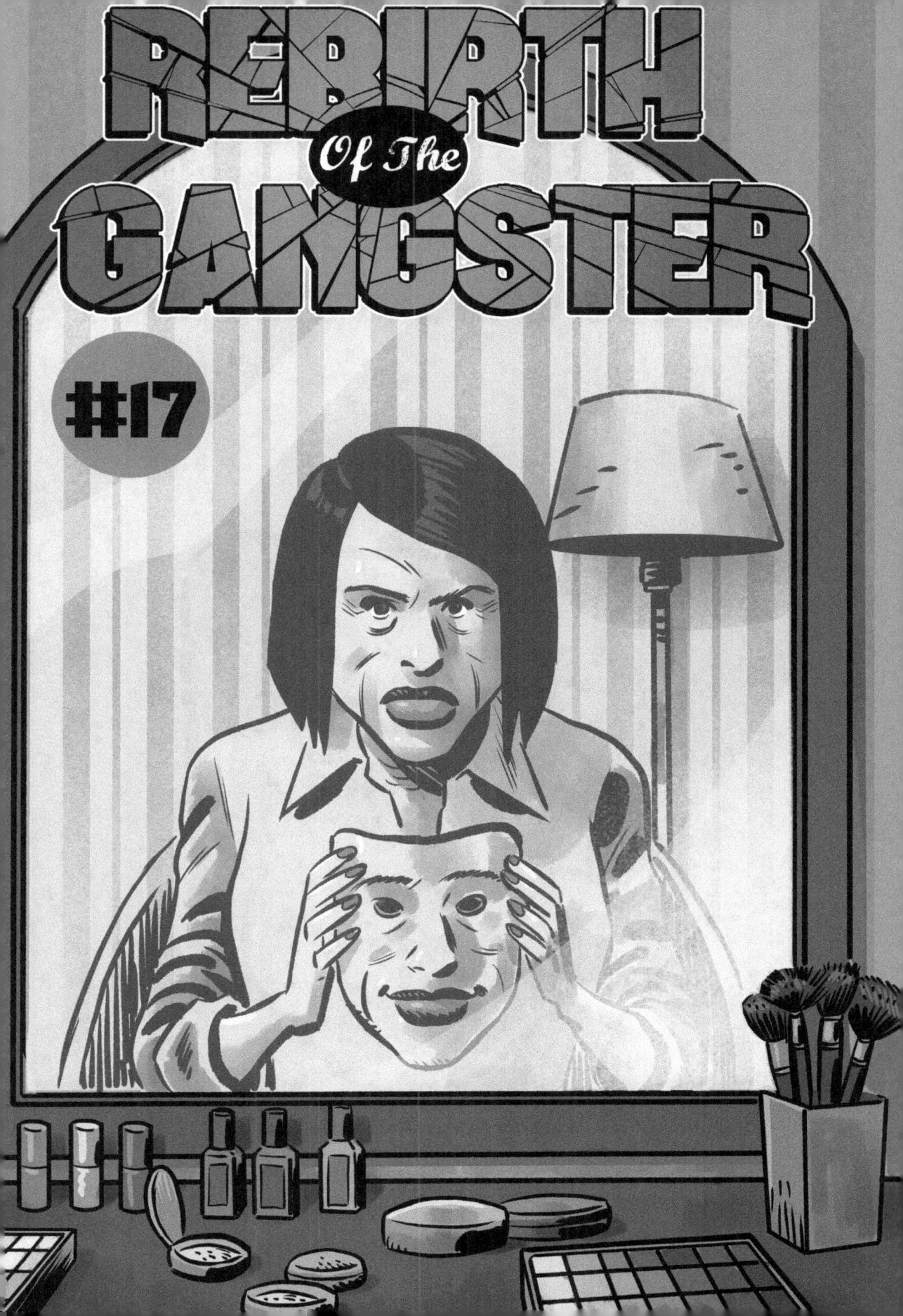

REBIRTH Of The GANGSTER

A Family Affair: Andrea

WHAT DO WE DO?

WE CAN'T LET MY DAD TURN US IN.

NATIONAL
YOUTH
ADVOCATE
PROGRAM

CLICK

SEND

HEY, GIRL! GOOD TO SEE YOU AGAIN!

YOU TOO. BETSY, I WANT YOU TO MEET A NEW FRIEND, RYAN.

RYAN, THIS IS MY OLD FRIEND, BETSY.

NICE TO MEET YOU -- RYAN!

AND, LINDA-- *OLD* FRIEND?

I'M NOT OLD, JUST EXPERIENCED.

SO, RYAN, HOW DO YOU KNOW THIS FIREBRAND?

WE MET DURING A MEETING.

YEAH, WE MET AT A MEETING AND HAVE HUNG OUT A LITTLE SINCE.

BUT I DON'T THINK I'M GOING RAFTING AGAIN AFTER LAST TIME!

RAFTING? SINCE WHEN DO YOU DO OUTDOORSY STUFF?

JUST RECENTLY, ONE TIME.

I'M JUST TRYING SOME NEW THINGS LATELY.

JUST LIKE US THREE NOW, HANGING OUT TOGETHER FOR THE FIRST TIME!

WHAT DO YOU MEAN?

I MEAN, WE USED TO TALK.

ACTUALLY TALK.

"WE USED TO HAVE FUN."

WE USED TO... MAKE LOVE MORE OFTEN.

--ACTING JUST LIKE KARISSA.

HAH! SHE WAS WILD WASN'T SHE?

KARISSA?

UH, JUST A FRIEND FROM BACK IN THE DAY.

YEAH, IT'S COMPLICATED. YOU'D HAVE TO *BE THERE.*

THANKS, MISTER. MY DAD AND I ARE PLAYING BASEBALL.

WHAT ARE YOU PLAYING?

THANKS.

...

HERE.

PUT THIS AWAY-- I WON'T BE WORKING ON THESE FOR A WHILE.

HEY, HON. WHAT'S UP?

HEY, MOM, I WAS HOPING I COULD ASK YOU A FEW QUESTIONS ABOUT GRANDPA.

UH, YOUR GRANDPA. WHY?

JUST... I DON'T KNOW MUCH ABOUT HIM.

IT'S TOO BAD HE DIED RIGHT WHEN I WAS BORN.

I KNOW, HONEY.

"I WISH YOU COULD'VE MET HIM.

DID DAD AND HIM GET ALONG?

WHAT?

WHY DO YOU ASK?

OH...I THOUGHT I HEARD DAD SAY SOMETHING ABOUT IT BEFORE.

NO, THEY GOT ALONG. EXCEPT...

"YOUR DAD HAD TO STAND UP TO HIM FOR ME."

WHAT'D GRANDPA HAVE AGAINST YOU?

OH, I USED TO RAISE A LITTLE HELL.

BUT I'VE GOTTA GO MEET SOMEONE. TALK TO YOU ABOUT THIS LATER?

HEY.

HEY!

THANKS FOR MEETING ME.

YEAH, WELL...

I'M HERE.

I JUST WANT TO START WITH--

I'M DONE WITH THAT STUFF.

TCH!

JUST... JUST HEAR ME OUT.

WHAT CAN I GET YOU, MISS?
JUST A COFFEE.
ANYTHING ELSE?
NO, THAT'S ALL--I WON'T BE HERE LONG.
I KNOW WHAT YOU'RE THINKING: THAT'S WHAT I SAID BEFORE.
SO WHAT'S CHANGED?
...
I THINK IT'S THAT I DIDN'T HAVE A GOAL.
I WASN'T AIMING FOR A JOB THAT WAS CALLING ME, SO I WASN'T WILLING TO PUT IN THE WORK.
BUT THAT'S CHANGED.
WHAT'S THIS?
SPEAKING TO YOUR CLASS...IT WAS THE FIRST THING THAT MADE ME FEEL ALIVE SINCE GETTING OUT OF PRISON.
AND I THOUGHT, "WHAT CAN I DO TO FEEL THAT WAY SOME MORE?"
HERE'S YOUR COFFEE, MISS.
THANKS. AND CAN I ACTUALLY GET THAT MENU?
I'LL BE STAYING LONGER THAN I THOUGHT...

A Family Affair: Marcus

"WHO DID?"

RINGGGG
RINGGGGG

YOU'VE REACHED CURTIS THOMPSON. PLEASE LEAVE YOUR NAME, YOUR NUMBER, AND A BRIEF MESSAGE, AND I'LL GET BACK TO YOU AS SOON AS I CAN. THANKS!

BEEP

HEY, HON. JUST CHECKING IN AND--

IT'S A SHAME BETSY COULDN'T JOIN US FOR DINNER TOO.

YEAH, I'M SURPRISED SHE DIDN'T JOIN.

WELL, SHE DIDN'T SEEM TOO THRILLED ABOUT US SPENDING TIME TOGETHER.

YEAH...

YEAH, IT'S LIKE SHE WANTS ME TO BE THE SAME LINDA SHE GREW UP WITH. BUT THAT'S THE PERSON WHO BECAME AN ADDICT.

I HEAR YA.

WHEN I GOT CLEAN, I FOUND OUT WHO MY REAL FRIENDS WERE. THE ONES WHO TRULY SUPPORTED ME CHANGING.

BUT WE CAN'T BE HELD BACK BY THOSE WHO DON'T WANT US TO CHANGE.

"ESPECIALLY IF THEY'RE CLOSE TO US AND WANT TO DRAG US DOWN WITH THEM."

BACKING OUT NOW, DENNIS?

HUNTER, YOU BELIEVE THIS SHIT?

WHAT ARE YOU GONNA DO ABOUT IT, *BOSS*?

WE GOTTA APPROACH THIS CAREFULLY...

BULLSHIT!

WE JUST GOTTA SLAP SOME SENSE INTO THIS PUSSY.

AND I DON'T WANT ONE MISTAKE TO, TO...

I WOULD IMPLICATE MYSELF JUST AS MUCH AS YOU IF I WENT TO THE COPS.

YOU'LL JUST CUT A DEAL.

NO, THAT WOULD DEFEAT THE POINT OF LEAVING THIS BEHIND.

YOU'LL JUST HAVE TO TRUST ME.

OH--IF ANYTHING HAPPENS TO ME, SOME RECORDINGS OF OUR "GAB SESSIONS" WILL BE SENT TO THE COPS.

SO YOU BETTER STAY AWAY.

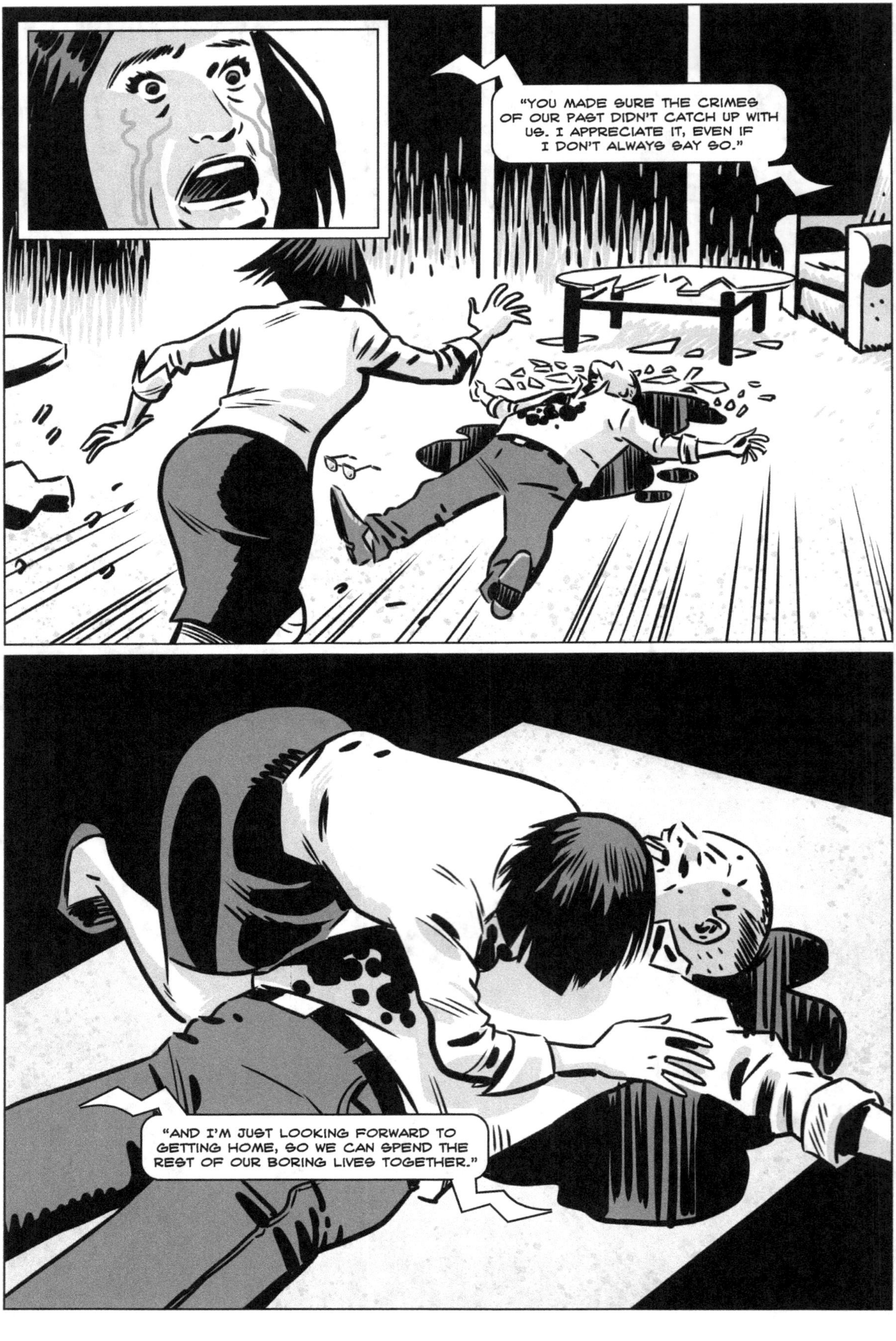
"YOU MADE SURE THE CRIMES OF OUR PAST DIDN'T CATCH UP WITH US. I APPRECIATE IT, EVEN IF I DON'T ALWAYS SAY SO."
"AND I'M JUST LOOKING FORWARD TO GETTING HOME, SO WE CAN SPEND THE REST OF OUR BORING LIVES TOGETHER."

Rebirth of the Gangster concludes in *Act 4: Inheritance*

www.ingramcontent.com/pod-product-compliance
Lightning Source LLC
Chambersburg PA
CBHW081919130726
47909CB00015B/3032